Oh please, let it be dandruff.

Suddenly, my heart started beating faster.

What if it was lice?

I could feel my face burning up. I was so embarrassed!

Harry moved in. He started looking closely at my scalp, parting strands of hair with his fingers. "Looks like their natural habitat is your head, Dougo."

Mrs. Flaubert approached our picnic table. "What's going on, boys? I thought we were observing bugs in our new nature center."

Harry looked up. "We are. I just found two tiny ones in Doug's hair."

...RRY
and the Battle of the Bugs

BY SUZY KLINE
PICTURES BY AMY WUMMER

PUFFIN BOOKS

PUFFIN BOOKS
An imprint of Penguin Random House LLC
375 Hudson Street
New York, New York 10014

First published in the United States of America by Viking,
an imprint of Penguin Random House LLC, 2017
Published by Puffin Books, an imprint of Penguin Random House LLC, 2018

THE LIBRARY OF CONGRESS HAS CATALOGED THE VIKING EDITION AS FOLLOWS:
Names: Kline, Suzy, author. | Wummer, Amy, illustrator.
Title: Horrible Harry and the battle of the bugs / by Suzy Kline ; illustrations
by Amy Wummer. Description: New York : VIKING, Published by Penguin
Group, [2017] | Series: Horrible Harry | Summary: "Doug is infested with
the one creepy-crawly thing Harry hates: lice! Will Harry be able to help
Doug get rid of them, or will Doug have to pack up and move
to a new country instead?"— Provided by publisher.
Identifiers: LCCN 2016053383 | ISBN 9780425288207 (hardcover)
Subjects: | CYAC: Lice—Fiction. | Friendship—Fiction.
Classification: LCC PZ7.K6797 Hnh 2017 | DDC [Fic]—dc23
LC record available at https://lccn.loc.gov/2016053383

Puffin Books ISBN 9780425288221

Printed in the United States of America

1 3 5 7 9 10 8 6 4 2

DEDICATED TO
the millions of children in the United States
who get lice every year and are embarrassed
about it, and to the school nurses who make
a real difference in a child's life by just being
kind and helpful.

Special appreciation to . . .

the National Association of School Nurses (nasn.org) and the American Academy of Pediatrics (healthychildren.org) for their helpful websites; my husband, Rufus, for his encouragement and wisdom; and most of all, my hardworking editor, Leila Sales, for her valuable help!

HORRIBLE HARRY
and the Battle of the Bugs

Contents

Bug Partners

My name is Doug and I'm in third grade at South School. Usually I write stories about my best friend Harry and the creepy-crawly things he loves, like ants, Edward the earwig, and Charles, his pet spider.

This time my story is different. It is about the *one* creepy-crawly thing that Harry hates and how he declared a battle against it!

It all started when we were outside in the new nature center next to our school. Miss Mackle—I mean, Mrs. Flaubert (I have to remember her new married name)—exclaimed, "Isn't this wonderful! We have our own science lab right here in this empty lot!"

"Can we climb a tree?" Sid asked.

"No," the teacher replied firmly, "but you can look closely at the bark for bugs. We are going to discover so many living things here!"

Harry took out his magnifying necklace. "Hey, guys! There's one right here on this oak tree. A beetle!"

Lots of kids joined Harry to watch the black bug scurry along.

I took a step back. Bugs are not my favorite thing!

Mrs. Flaubert passed out plastic magnifying glasses to all of us. "See how many different bugs you can find. Observe them, and jot down in your notebook where you find them. Do a quick sketch of their habitat—the natural home where each bug lives. When we get back to the classroom, we'll see if we can identify some of the insects just like real scientists do."

"Real scientists!" Mary exclaimed. "Can we work with a partner?" she asked, looking over at Ida and Song Lee.

"I had the same thought," the teacher replied. "You can collaborate with each other!" She took a piece of paper from her pocket. "I picked names out of the glass jar on my desk to make a list of bug partners for our entomology studies."

"What's that?" Sid asked.

"The study of insects," Mary answered. "We learned that in second grade when we visited the pond with Professor Guo. He was an entomologist. He studied insects in their natural habitats!"

"Oh yeah!" Sid exclaimed. "I remember now!"

"Yes!" the teacher replied. "We are being entomologists when we study insects."

Harry was still watching that black beetle. He has been an entomologist his whole life!

"Sidney and ZuZu, you'll be partners," the teacher began. The two boys immediately started looking for insects on an old log.

"Harry and Song Lee," Mrs. Flaubert

called out. Harry suddenly stopped looking at that black bug and turned around. He flashed a toothy smile at Song Lee. Song Lee smiled back. Harry has liked her ever since kindergarten, when she brought in a potato beetle for show-and-tell.

"Dexter and Ida," the teacher continued. Ida did a pirouette on one foot, spinning around in the dirt. She takes ballet. When Dexter heard her name, he pretended to strum a guitar. He loves Elvis! I could tell they were happy about being partners.

When Mrs. Flaubert got to the very end, Mary and I were left standing there. "And you two!" she concluded, smiling again.

"Great!" Mary replied. "Come on,

Doug, we need to find a beautiful insect. Don't touch it though," she warned. "Some bite!"

I rolled my eyes. Working with Mary was like teaming up with the school principal.

"Is there such a thing as a *beautiful* bug?" I asked.

"Of course!" Mary insisted. "Come on, Doug, follow me."

Mary was smart but *very* bossy.

So how bad could things get?

I found out half an hour later!

The Bug Harry Hates

Mary and I were sitting next to each other at one of the picnic tables in the nature center, drawing butterflies. "Be sure to include the milkweed plant," Mary coached. Then she pointed to the green leaves I was drawing. "You don't have any flowers or cream-colored eggs. You have to put those in, Doug. That's why the monarch butterfly goes to a milkweed plant—to get nectar and lay her eggs."

I sighed. I didn't feel like drawing flowers or eggs. When I looked up, I could see Harry and Song Lee looking for more bugs near our table.

"Hey, Dougo," Harry said. He was standing right behind me now. "I just spotted a tiny bug!"

"Yeah?" I said. I reached for the blue crayon.

Mary snatched it out of my hand and handed me a purple one. "You have to make the flowers a violet color," she ordered.

"I was putting in the sky!" I snapped.

"You're supposed to be an entomologist, Doug! They don't color in the sky when they're drawing a habitat!"

I put the crayon down. I needed a break from Mary! "What new bug did you see, Harry?" I said.

"It's a minuscule bugger about the size of a sesame seed."

"No kidding?" I replied. "Good thing you have a magnifying glass."

"Where is it?" Song Lee asked.

"Right here in Doug's hair."

"What?" I exclaimed.

Mary looked worried.

"Get it off!" I said, not moving an inch.

Suddenly, my heart started beating faster.

What if it was lice?

I could feel my face burning up. I was so embarrassed!

Harry moved in. He started looking closely at my scalp, parting strands of hair with his fingers. "Looks like their natural habitat is your head, Dougo."

Mrs. Flaubert approached our picnic table. "What's going on, boys? I thought we were observing bugs in our new nature center."

Harry looked up. "We are. I just found two tiny ones in Doug's hair."

"T-t-two?" I stuttered.

When I looked at the teacher it was

hard to focus. My eyes were filling up with water.

Mrs. Flaubert patted my shoulder. "Don't worry, Doug. I'll have the school nurse take a look. It may just be dandruff."

"Or the one bug that I hate," Harry whispered.

Oh please, I thought. *Let it be dandruff!*

The Guillotine

I asked if Harry could go with me to the nurse's office, but the teacher said no.

So I walked down the hall alone toward the little room at the end. I felt like I was going to the guillotine! But, I realized as I thought about it more, if I *did* get my head chopped off, I wouldn't have lice anymore!

That made me laugh out loud!

For about two seconds.

"Hi, Doug," the school nurse said when I appeared at her door. She likes to wear blouses with fruit on them. Today it was clumps of red grapes. She smelled like soap.

"Hello, Mrs. Cherry," I said, moaning.

Suddenly, Harry popped up in the doorway. He had a note in his hand. "My head started itching," he said, "so Mrs. Flaubert said for me to come, too."

When Harry winked, I gave him a nod. We both knew he was faking it.

"Mary said she doesn't want to be your bug partner anymore," Harry told me. "She thinks you have lice. You can work with Song Lee and me, Dougo!"

That brought some relief. I'd rather not work with Mary!

"I think it's time for me to visit your class," Mrs. Cherry replied. "I need to clear up some misunderstandings about head lice."

I was hoping to be in Timbuktu then.

After Mrs. Cherry examined my head, she examined Harry's. I could watch her better when she did his. She pulled strands of hair apart, then looked closely at the scalp behind his ears and just above his neck.

As soon as she was finished, she started tapping a number on the telephone. "I didn't see any lice on your head, Harry, but I did find some nits, or lice eggs, on yours, Doug."

Oh no! I had lice!

The nurse looked at me. "Does your head itch?"

"No. I don't feel anything."

"Some people don't. Others itch. Some people have trouble sleeping and are irritable when they get lice."

"Doug's been a grouch!" Harry joked.

I just rolled my eyes while Mrs. Cherry put the phone to her ear.

She talked to my mom about the situation, then handed the receiver to me. "She wants to talk with you, Doug."

"Mom?" I said.

"Honey, I'm so sorry you got lice. But no worries, I can treat it when you come home. It will all come out in the wash. How are you feeling?"

"Nothing hurts. I can't even feel the lice on my head. But I feel lousy," I moaned.

"Speaking of lousy," Harry piped up, "did you know one lice *is* a louse?"

I sank down further into my chair. "Can I come home, Mom, *now*?" I asked.

Then the lunch bell rang.

"The nurse said you could finish your school day, dear," she replied. "She doesn't want you to miss any schoolwork. I'll call the doctor and ask him what shampoo I should use. We can take care of the problem right after school, but if you're uncomfortable, Mrs. Cherry also said I could come and get you earlier."

"I am not going to be comfortable until I get those nits out of my hair!" I said.

"Then I'll pick you up in an hour, Doug. I may have to stop by the pharmacy first."

I handed the phone back to the nurse. After she and my mom exchanged a few words, Mrs. Cherry hung up.

"Why don't you and Harry go have lunch in the cafeteria? After you have a bite to eat, you can get your things and wait for your mom in the office. Just don't have any head-to-head contact with anyone, because that will spread the lice."

"I won't!" I said.

When we got out into the hallway, Harry spoke first. "It's a bummer that you're going home, Dougo. You'll miss doing the bug research this afternoon."

"No problem, Harry," I replied. "I'm taking the bugs with me. I have my own science lab on my head."

When we both laughed, it felt kind of good.

"Look," Harry said. "I'll come over after school and we can both battle the bugs together! I have a special weapon I can use."

"Sounds good," I said. "I'll be waiting for you."

As we walked into the cafeteria, we spotted Room 3B's table. As soon as Mary saw us coming, she started whispering to her friends.

At that moment, I wanted to disappear from South School!

Cafeteria Doom

The cafeteria was serving mac and cheese. Ordinarily that's one of my favorites. But today was different. I was in such a gloomy mood, I didn't even care.

"Big helping, please," Harry said as we scooted our trays along the lunch line.

Mrs. Funderburke, the head cook, had oven mitts on and was taking another tray out of the oven. "I made plenty," she said with a big smile. "How are you boys today?"

"Great!" Harry said. "I like your apron!"

Mrs. Funderburke beamed. Harry is her favorite.

"How about you, Doug?" the cook asked.

I just shrugged. I didn't feel like talking.

"He just came down with a bug," Harry said.

I jabbed him in the ribs.

"I hope it's not a cold," the cook replied.

"No, a bad mood bit him," Harry explained.

When Mrs. Funderburke chuckled, I shot Harry a look.

"That happens to everyone, Doug," she said, giving me an extra helping of mac and cheese.

"Thanks," I said.

When we left the kitchen, I whispered to Harry, "I don't want to talk about it! Don't bring it up again. And definitely don't say *the L word*."

"I won't," Harry agreed.

As soon as we sat down, Mary moved

over so she wouldn't have to sit next to us. Sydney and Ida and Dexter and ZuZu joined her.

I understood why they moved down. I probably would have done the same thing if someone near me had lice. But it still made me feel bad.

Mary leaned forward and made a face at me and Harry. "I bet you *both* have lice. You two are best friends. *Eweyee, eweyee.* You should eat in the hallway."

Song Lee stayed where she was and kept eating her kimchee across from us with a plastic spoon. "I got lice in first grade," she said. "My little sister got it, too. My mom was able to get the nits out of my hair with a tiny comb. It was no fun."

It was good to know I wasn't the only

one on planet Earth who had it.

Harry had a mouth full of mac and cheese when Mrs. Funderburke stopped by our table. "How are you all doing?" she asked.

"Good!" lots of kids replied.

Mary waved at the cook. "The only time I eat hot lunch is on mac-and-cheese day," she called out. "Your recipe is better than my mom's."

"You're so thoughtful, Mary," the cook replied.

Yeah, I thought. *Real* thoughtful.

"I brought some extra Parmesan cheese, kids," the cook said. "Help yourself!"

She passed it to me first. "Thanks," I said.

I sprinkled a little on and then

handed the container to Harry. After he dumped a mountain of that cheese on his macaroni, he slid the plastic container down the table to Mary's group.

Mary immediately leaned back. "Don't touch it, guys," she whispered, "or you'll get lice, too!"

Sid and Ida obeyed. Dexter pushed it back with a napkin.

That's when I knew going to Timbuktu wouldn't be far enough. I had to go to Siberia.

After the cook left, Song Lee stared at Mary. She was whispering something in Ida's ear. Then she looked at me and laughed.

Song Lee stood up. "Mary!" she scolded. "You are being mean! When I got lice, I felt bad, but the worst part

was having people like *you* make fun of
me. That's not being a friend! What if it
happened to you?"

Mary blew up her bangs in a huff. "It
wouldn't happen to me!" she snapped. "I
always keep my hair clean!"

When Song Lee sat down, no one
said another word.

Everyone just ate their lunch.
Silently.

Ten minutes later, the bell rang, and kids headed outside for the playground. Song Lee lingered with Harry and me.

As the three of us walked slowly up the stairs together, I realized how great it was to have two loyal friends.

The Battle Begins

Mom picked me up shortly after lunch. When we got home, she washed my hair in the kitchen sink with a special shampoo the doctor had prescribed. She used a tiny comb to get the nits, or eggs, off each strand of my hair. "They like to be near your scalp," she told me.

I kept my eyes closed. The whole thing grossed me out!

When there were a familiar three

knocks on the back door, Mom called out, "Come in!" Her hands were soapy.

"Hey, Dougo!" Harry said as he bounced in. "How's it going?"

"Slow!" Mom answered. "It's a long and tedious process. *Real* nitpicking!" She giggled.

"Very funny, Mom." I groaned. "Thanks for coming over, Harry."

"Hey, this is where the action is!" Harry exclaimed. "It's time to begin the battle of the bugs!"

That made me smile for the first time that afternoon.

"I brought my special weapon: Grandma Spooger's terminator comb!" Harry said. "It has really thin silvery teeth." He pulled it out of his pocket and handed it to Mom. "Grandma told me to tell you she just washed it in very hot water to make sure it's completely clean."

"Thanks, Harry!" Mom chuckled. "So you had lice, too?"

"Oh yeah!" Harry replied. "I got it three times one summer after camp! You didn't know me then."

"Three times?" I said.

"Yup! Grandma finally saved enough money to buy that terminator comb. It's metal and lasts forever. She didn't want to use the lice shampoo because it has chemicals in it. She used mayonnaise instead."

"Mayonnaise? No kidding, Harry?" I said.

"Yup! My cousin used olive oil when he got lice, but we didn't have any. The mayonnaise was kind of neat, actually. It felt so silky smooth on my scalp. I kept a shower cap on my head for a couple of hours. We smothered those buggers! You should have seen all the nits and dead lice she combed out with that weapon! I think that's when I first got interested in bugs."

It made me kind of sick. I didn't think I'd ever want to put mayonnaise on my sandwich again.

"Fascinating, Harry," Mom said, handing him back his comb. "I'll do this side of Doug's head, and you can do the other."

"Aye aye, captain!" he replied. "It's time to go to battle!"

Mom chuckled. "Thanks, Harry. Humor helps!"

Harry flashed a toothy smile, then got to work. He used his magnifying necklace to look closely at my scalp. "Every time I spot a nit," he said, "I use my metal comb like a sword and spear that bugger away from a strand of hair." When he blotted the comb onto a paper towel, I could see some of the teeny tiny nits. They were yellowish tan or white.

"I think I'll get a magnifying glass, too," Mom said. "You're making better progress than me, Harry!"

It took more than an hour to comb my whole head. Finally, Mom used the sink sprayer to rinse out my hair and then dried my head with a towel.

"How about some ice cream, boys?" she said.

"Yeah!" Harry blurted out.

Mom scooped chocolate and strawberry ice cream into cones for Harry and me.

As we were licking them in the kitchen, I was thinking how good it was to be home, and to have Harry over.

I decided that I was never returning to school.

And then the phone rang.

"It's for you, Doug," Mom said. "It's Song Lee."

I took the phone in my left hand because I had my ice-cream cone in the other.

"How's it going?" Song Lee asked.

"Well, today's treatment is done," I said. "The doctor said we have to do one more in ten days just to be sure we didn't miss a single live egg and have another round of lice start."

"But the hard part is over," she said.

"No," I said. "The hard part is returning to school."

"I know," she said. "I wanted to go back to South Korea."

"Well, I'm looking at Siberia."

When we both laughed, Mom gave me a concerned look.

"Thanks for calling, Song Lee," I said.

My mom patted me on the head as

I hung up. "I'm taking you to school tomorrow, dear," she said. "I want Mrs. Cherry to check your hair after our treatment today."

I just groaned. I didn't mind seeing Mrs. Cherry anymore. She was nice. But I didn't want to go back to school. What if the kids were still whispering about me?

Harry swallowed his last bite of ice cream, then grabbed my wiffle ball and bat next to the back door. "Time to play ball, Dougo!"

"You're right," I replied. I felt like whacking something.

The Nurse's Room

The next morning, Mom wouldn't let me go to Siberia. She said it was too far away.

She forced me to get into the car.

"How about Timbuktu?" I said. "It's a little closer."

"Douglas, it costs thousands of dollars to fly round trip to those places. It costs ninety cents for gas to get to school."

I needed to rob a bank.

"This will all be over soon, dear, and next week everyone will forget what happened!"

"Oh yeah, sure!" I grumbled.

Mom tried to change the subject. "I packed some banana bread in your lunch. And some grapes. You like those."

I didn't want to think about fruit right now. It reminded me of the nurse's office and being back at school.

Mom parked the car by the playground just as the bell was ringing. I could see my friends in a tight huddle at the kickball diamond. There were kids from other classes joining them. Usually I'd be in there with them. I wondered if *that* was how I got my lice. From someone else's head in that huddle.

After we entered the main doors, we walked down the hall to the nurse's little room. Mrs. Cherry greeted us at the door. Today her blouse had blueberries on it.

When I sat down, she examined the back of my neck, and the hair behind my ears.

"Great job," she said. "It's hard to get every single nit, but you got the ones close to the scalp. There are only one or two down farther along the hair shaft that are just dead eggs. They'll eventually wash out."

Mom sighed. "Oh, good."

Then Mrs. Cherry added, "I'll be talking with Mrs. Flaubert's class this morning. I want to make sure the kids are not uptight and anxious about lice."

"Thank you!" Mom said. Then she gave me a kiss and left. I wanted to go with her. But she insisted I stay at school and wait for "the L talk."

The L Talk

It came about ten thirty that morning. The L Talk.

My class turned quiet when Mrs. Cherry began speaking. "Some of you may know we've had a few cases of lice at our school."

The only ones who looked at me were Ida, Sid, Dexter, and ZuZu. Mary was not there. That was a relief!

Mrs. Cherry continued. "There is no

need to panic. Lice is treatable. There are special shampoos and fine-toothed combs that can help you and your parents get rid of it. The lice do not spread any kind of disease. They are just pesky bugs that can only crawl. If you don't have head-to-head contact with other people, you won't get it. The important thing is to remain calm, and be understanding toward someone who has it. The worst thing is to tease someone about it."

Yes! I thought. I wished Mary had heard that message!

Mrs. Flaubert went to the front of the room with the nurse. "If any of you entomologists want to learn more about lice, Mrs. Michaelsen, our librarian, has offered to do a special study group in the library today."

Harry and Song Lee immediately raised their hands. I had to think about it.

Then Mrs. Cherry asked if there were any questions.

"What if I keep my hair clean?" ZuZu asked.

"Getting head lice is no reflection on your own personal hygiene," Miss Cherry explained. "People who are very neat and clean get it, too."

"Can you get it from a jar of Parmesan cheese?" Sid asked.

When some kids giggled, the nurse smiled. "I'm glad you asked that, Sidney," Mrs. Cherry replied. "There are a lot of crazy ideas about lice. But in order to survive, a louse must stay on a human scalp. That's where it gets its blood supply to live. It doesn't care about cheese."

"How do you get it, then?" ZuZu asked.

"From head-to-head contact," the nurse said.

"What about sharing combs or hair ribbons?" Ida asked.

"Or sharing hats?" ZuZu added.

"It's not a good idea to do that," Mrs. Cherry explained. "So be extra safe, and don't."

Then she passed out pamphlets about lice that had more information, and left.

Afterward, the class worked on identifying the insects we'd found in our nature center yesterday. When Harry and Song Lee pushed their desks together, I stopped by to see what they were doing. They were sketching an insect on a big piece of paper. It was a picture of one louse crawling out of its egg on a strand of hair. They were adding facts from the nurse's pamphlet.

Mrs. Flaubert came over. "Doug? Would you like to join Harry and Song Lee?"

"Okay," I said.

"Great!" the teacher replied.

When I returned to my desk to get my pencil kit, there was a note on top. It was decorated with monarch butterflies.

After I read it, I looked across the aisle at Ida and said, "Nice butterflies." She smiled.

I survived that first day back. I was glad I didn't rob a bank or go to another continent. ZuZu, Dexter, Sidney, and Ida even joined Harry, Song Lee, and me for lunch, just like usual.

The best part was that the three of us collected some important facts about lice. Mrs. Michaelsen, the librarian, helped us a lot. She showed us some websites to go to for information. She was so impressed with our hard work and research that she suggested we do a science project about head lice for the county science fair!

Up until the last five minutes of our school day, I was starting to feel good.

And then Mrs. Flaubert came to my desk and asked me to do something.

Going to Mary's House

It was just before the dismissal bell that the teacher appeared at my desk. "Doug, Mary's mother called and asked if you could drop by her house with Mary's homework. She said you live just around the corner."

Oh man, I thought. *Are you kidding? Go to Mary's house? She probably wouldn't want to touch the papers I brought.*

I didn't answer.

Song Lee and Harry did for me.

"I can go with you," Harry said.

"Me too," Song Lee added.

"What a good idea, kids!" the teacher exclaimed. "Mary needs some cheering up after being home sick."

I took Mary's folder of papers from the teacher, but I wasn't happy about it. Mrs. Flaubert had clipped a note on the front with a smiley face.

"Thanks," the teacher said, and then she called out, "Okay, class, time to get your things together and line up."

After the final bell rang, the three of us made our way to Mary's house. I carried her pile of papers. It included her bug journal and that pamphlet the nurse had handed out.

"Thanks for coming with me, guys," I said.

"We have to stick together," Harry replied.

"That's what friends do," Song Lee agreed.

After turning the corner, we were on Mary's street. Her green-and-white house was the biggest one on the block. As we got closer, we could see her yard was perfectly mowed. Rosebushes of every color lined her walkway. Her mailbox was huge. There were even bird feeders and a birdbath.

When we walked up the steps onto the wide porch, there was a swing with flowered pillows.

Harry rang the doorbell.

"Nice-sounding chimes," Song Lee said.

Mrs. Berg showed up right away. "Oh, thanks for stopping by with Mary's papers."

"How is she?" Song Lee asked.

"Very tired. She didn't sleep well last night. I'm letting her rest today."

"MOM!" Mary screamed from the top of the stairs.

Mrs. Berg looked embarrassed. "She is very irritable. I don't know what's the matter," she said.

When Mary appeared at the bottom of the stairwell, she was scratching her head.

"You might want to read the pamphlet from the nurse," I said. "She came to our classroom today to talk about . . . head lice."

Harry patted me on the back. I'd finally said the L word. Now that it was my science project, I figured I shouldn't be scared of saying it anymore.

"Oh dear! *Head lice!*" Mrs. Berg groaned. "I remember my brother getting that when we were growing up. Then I got it! Well, there are a lot worse things that could happen."

Mrs. Berg was very understanding.

"MOM! WHAT ARE YOU TALKING ABOUT?" Mary screamed again. "*You* had lice?"

When Mrs. Berg turned around to look at Mary, she noticed her scratching. "Does your head itch, dear?" she asked. Mary took off upstairs.

"I think I better check on things,"

Mrs. Berg said. Then she gave us a wink. "Thanks, kids. See you later."

"Well, that was kind of fun," Harry said as we scooted down the steps. "Mary will find out what lice are like *if* she has them."

"Yeah." I grinned.

"I don't think she'll tease people about it anymore if she does," Song Lee said.

Halfway down the street, Harry stopped walking. "You know what?" he said. "I just figured out how you could *never* get lice ever!"

"How?" I asked.

"Just live by yourself the rest of your life. The only way you can get head lice is from head-to-head contact. There wouldn't be any other head around."

As we continued walking, we all thought about it.

"I think I'd rather risk it, and hang out with you guys," I said.

"Me too," Harry and Song Lee agreed.

It All Comes Out in the Wash

Mary did have head lice.

She had a professional come to her house to do the hair treatment. She also put her stuffed animals in a plastic bag for two weeks, and washed all her brushes, combs, and bed linens in hot water. I was glad Mary returned to class the next day. I felt kind of bad for her.

When Mary saw me, she came over right away.

"I'm mad at you, Doug!" she snarled. "You gave me lice!"

"What? You think you got it from *me*?" I replied.

"Yes, I do! Maybe from one of our kickball huddles, or when we were working on our bug project together. That's when I had head-to-head contact with you."

"Well, maybe I got it from *you*, Mare!" I snarled back. "Did you ever think of that?"

Mary didn't have an answer for me.

"How do we know we didn't both get it from someone else in that kickball huddle? Lots of kids join us at recess from all grades," I said.

"I guess we never really will know for sure," Mary said thoughtfully.

"No, we won't," I replied.

Then Mary changed her tone of voice. "I shouldn't have teased you or whispered about you, Doug. That was mean. I wouldn't like it if someone made fun of me for having lice," she said. "I even thought touching a bottle of Parmesan cheese would give it to me! Really! Then I read that pamphlet Mrs. Cherry sent home about lice."

And that was when I knew we should include Mary. "Do you want to join Song Lee, Harry, and me to do a science project on lice? Mrs. Michaelsen is helping us find more information. She even said we could enter the project in the county science fair next month."

Mary beamed. "How exciting! We

could share our experiences with head lice and get out the real facts!"

Song Lee and Harry came over. "You're going to do it with us?" Harry asked.

"I'd love to," Mary replied. "It's my chance to be a real entomologist!"

"All right, Mare!" Harry said, slapping her five.

"We can save kids all over the world from the embarrassment of getting head lice," Mary continued. "They need to know it all comes out in the wash. Got lice? Shampoo and comb, comb, comb the nits away. Don't freak out like I did!" Mary was waving her hands in the air!

"We could mention some of the myths about head lice," I suggested. "Maybe that will help people realize the things about lice that aren't true!"

"Yes!" the girls replied.

"I know one myth I want to attack first," Mary said. "The idea that neat people don't get head lice."

"Yeah!" Harry added. "And I know one fact I want to add. Olive oil or mayonnaise can help get rid of the lice!"

Mary stared at Harry. "Really? You're going to mention *mayonnaise and olive oil* in our science project?"

Harry and I looked at each other and laughed. This was going to be fun!

Epilogue

We entered our head lice project in the county science fair and won third prize! Mr. Cardini, our principal, Mrs. Cherry, and Mrs. Flaubert came to the science fair with our parents, and they were all really proud. Mr. Cardini asked us to share our prize-winning science project with South School on the schoolwide morning TV show. He said we were very brave to talk openly about it. He also said that some people choose to keep it confidential, and that's okay, too.

Our trifold science project stayed in the library so kids could see it every day. It was like our fight against lice could continue on with our project.

The best part was what happened to us at recess the day after our TV show.

This fifth grader came up to us on the playground. "You don't know me," he said, "but I want to thank you guys for doing that science project on lice. I had it, too. I've never told anyone about it because I thought only losers got lice. Now I don't feel that way anymore. You four guys all had it, studied it, and won a prize about it at a science fair! That's so cool! Winners get lice, too. Thanks!" And he ran off.

"I feel like we just got a group hug from that kid!" I said.

"It was better than a group hug," Mary said. "Because there was no . . ."

Then she pointed to her head.

"Head-to-head contact!" Harry, Song Lee, and I chimed in.

And we all laughed.

Ten Important Questions About Head Lice

Question 1: How do you get head lice?

False: By touching someone who has lice or by using something that person used, like a pencil or Parmesan cheese.

True: By head-to-head contact or occasionally by sharing combs and hats with someone who has lice.

Question 2: How many children get head lice in the United States?

False: It is rare to get head lice.

True: Millions of children get head lice every year.

Question 3: What are lice?

False: Bugs that can fly and spread disease.

True: Tiny crawling insects about the size of a sesame seed that don't spread disease. Lice can't hop, jump, or fly. A single one is called a louse. It feeds on tiny amounts of blood only from human scalps.

Question 4: What are nits?

False: Bugs.

True: Lice eggs and their shell casings. They are usually yellow or white. Nits are attached with a sticky substance to the hair shaft.

Question 5: Who gets lice?

False: People with dirty hair and messy rooms. Neat people who wash their hair every day *never* get lice.

True: Anyone who has head-to-head contact with people who have lice can get it themselves, no matter how neat and clean they are.

Question 6: Do head lice make your head itch?

False: Yes. That's how you know if you have head lice. Your head itches.

True: Not always. Some people with lice itch; others don't.

Question 7: What should you do if you have lice?

False: Don't tell anyone. Ignore it!

True: Talk to a school nurse and your doctor.

Head lice can be treated at home by your parents with special shampoos and fine-toothed combs.

Question 8: What can you do to prevent head lice from returning?

False: Throw out all your bed linens, towels, brushes, combs, hats, and scarves.

True: Wash clothes, towels, hats, and bed linens in hot water and dry on high heat. Items you can't wash, like some stuffed animals, can be sealed in a plastic bag for two weeks. The lack of oxygen will kill any leftover nits.

Question 9: How should you act toward someone who has lice?

False: Make fun of them.

True: Be kind and understanding.

Question 10: What was the hardest part about having head lice for us?

False: It hurts to have someone comb out the nits.

True: Two things: getting whispered about when we returned to school, and feeling grossed out about having bugs in our hair!